My Super Soul Dad

Words by Bronny

Illustrations by Fievre

www.bronnysbooks.com

I've got a Soul Daddy
Sent from the Universe for me
Mummy said she asked for him
and the angels sent him as fast as can be

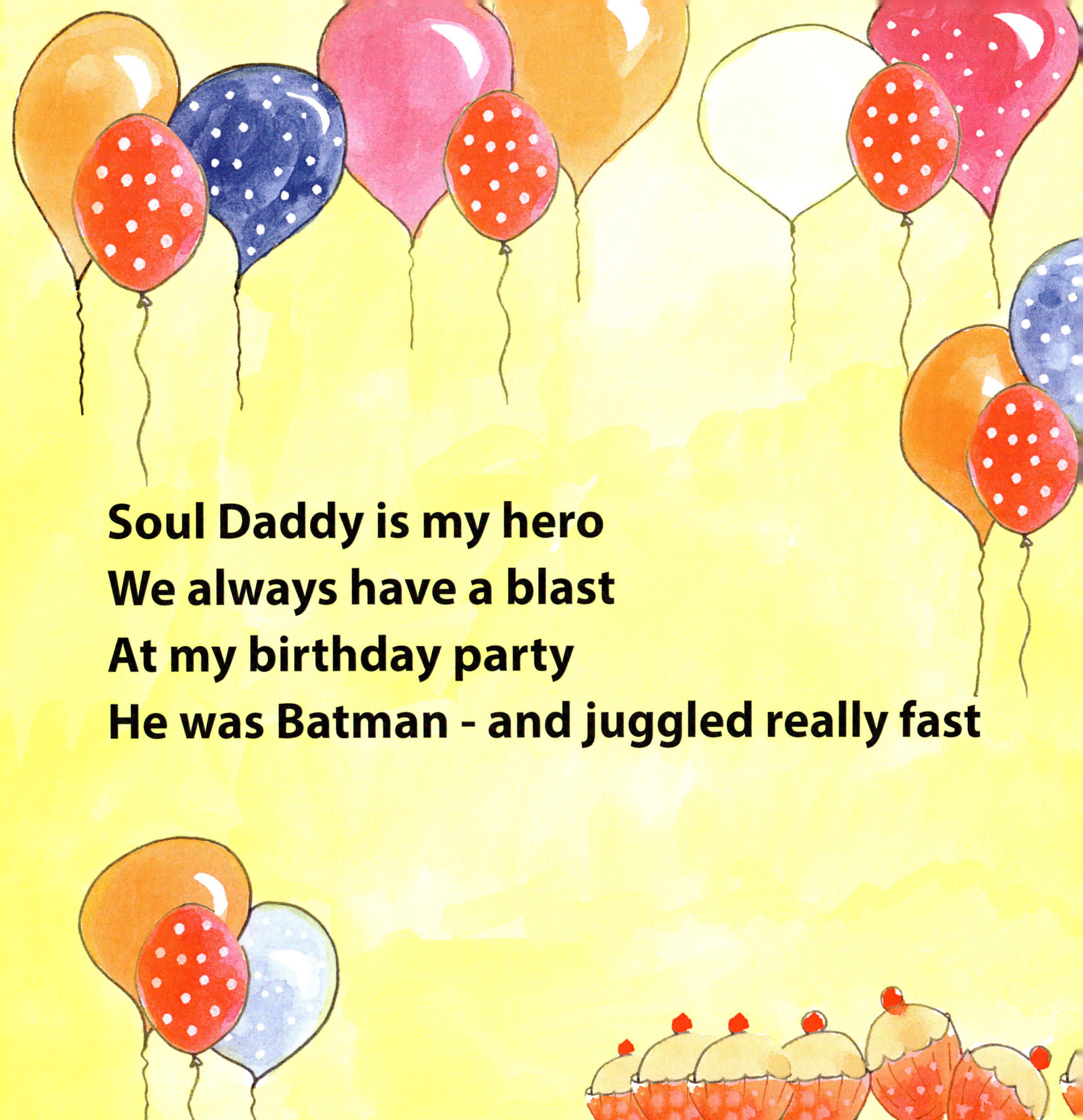

Soul Daddy is my hero
We always have a blast
At my birthday party
He was Batman - and juggled really fast

My Soul Dad builds bikes
And he taught me how to ride
The best weekends we all go out
And burn along seaside

One summer at the beach
A big crab pinched my toe
My Soul Daddy kissed it better
Then told that crab where to go

Some people call him my step dad
But mum says he's a dad for the soul
She said when my soul dad came along
He made our family whole

Mummy and Daddy are having a baby
They said he'll be my brother
I'm so excited and just can't wait
Because then we'll have each other

My Soul Dad is amazing
He's the absolute rocking best
He sings and dances around the house
In his shorts and vest

When mummy met my Soul Dad
I was as happy as can be
You see, that was the day
He became my Super Soul Daddy